What If the Teacher Calls on Me?

By Alan Gross
Illustrated by Mike Venezia

ᕉ CHILDRENS PRESS, CHICAGO

Library of Congress Cataloging in Publication Data

Gross, Alan, 1947-
    What if the teacher calls on me?

    SUMMARY: A child worries that he won't be able to give
the correct answer when the teacher calls on him in class.
    [1. School stories]   I. Venezia, Mike.   II. Title.
PZ7.G899Wh   [E]   79-18560
ISBN 0-516-03671-8

What if the teacher calls on me?

I hate being called on.

I get all mixed up.

5

And everybody's looking at me.

Even when I know the answer
I get mixed up,
  sometimes.

It's not the teacher's fault.
She tries.

She keeps asking me the question
  in different ways.
I know the question.
I don't know the answer.

So she says, "Well, tell us what you think."
I think I wish I were at home.

Or she keeps saying, "Do you understand?
    Do you understand?"
    So finally, I say, "Yes, I understand."
    But I don't—not really.

If you tell her you understand,
  then usually she lets you sit down.

Maybe something's wrong with me.
Other people seem to understand.

I know the other kids think I'm stupid.
They don't tell me. They just think it.

I'll bet they laugh at me. Call me names
behind my back.

They don't know how smart I am, inside.
I mean, I know stuff.

Sometimes, when the teacher calls on
someone else, I know the answer then.
I almost always do, almost.

She always seems to call on me when I'm not paying attention.

Oh, no.
She's asking a question now.

And here I was not listening again.

What if she calls on me?

The chances are 30 to 1 that she won't.

I'll just try to make myself look as
  small as possible.
Maybe she won't see me then.

Oh, no. She saw me.

I'll smile at her.
"Hello, there, teacher."

I know, I'll try to make myself look smart.
That way she won't think she caught me.

I'll even look as though I know the answer.
A knowing smile. A look of confidence.

I'll even raise my hand.

Or, I'll say, "I know. I know."
As if I'm bursting with the answer.

Oh, oh, I got it. Call on me, teacher!

Oh, no.
"Me? Um . . . ah,
    repeat the question, please?"

ABOUT THE AUTHOR AND ARTIST:

Alan Gross and Mike Venezia first met in 1970 while writing and designing television commercials for the Pillsbury Doughboy. They have also joined forces for Nestles Chocolate and many of the Kellogg's cereal brands. Both are native Chicagoans with solid backgrounds in children's advertising—good children's advertising, that is. Their first children's book was *Sometimes I Worry*.

Alan, the writer, studied journalism and creative writing at the University of Missouri. He dropped out of graduate school to be an actor. Three of his plays have been produced in Chicago, *Lunching, The Phone Room,* and *The Man in Room 605*.

Mike, the illustrator, graduated from The School of the Art Institute in Chicago. His paintings have been shown in various galleries around Chicago.